LE PONT

D'AVIGNON

MADELINE AND THE GYPSIES

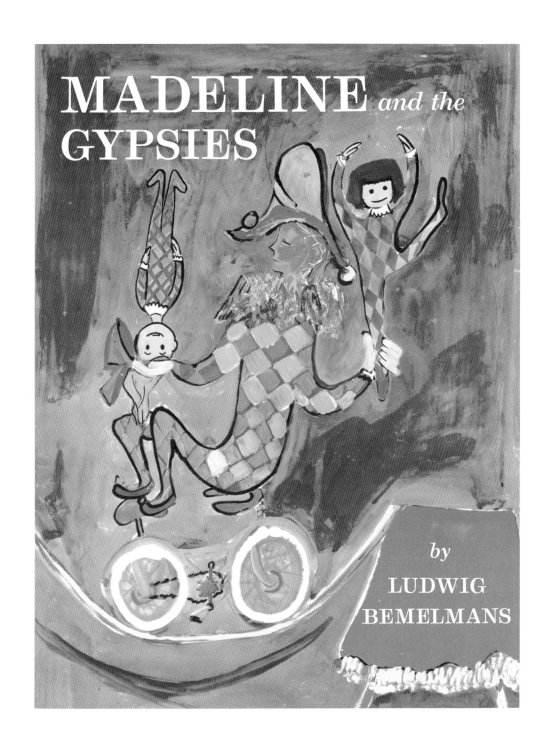

MADELINE *and the* GYPSIES

by
LUDWIG BEMELMANS

PUFFIN BOOKS

First published by The Viking Press 1959
Viking Seafarer Edition published 1973
Reprinted 1975
Published in Picture Puffins 1977
27 29 30 28

Copyright © Ludwig Bemelmans, 1958, 1959
Copyright renewed Madeleine Bemelmans and Barbara Bemelmans, 1986, 1987

Library of Congress Cataloging in Publication Data
Bemelmans, Ludwig, 1898–1962.   Madeline and the gypsies.
Summary: Pepito, son of the Spanish ambassador, and
Madeline, rescued by gypsies during a storm, travel and
perform with their wandering friends until they again
find Miss Clavel.
[1. Circus stories.   2. Gypsies—Fiction.
3. Stories in rhyme]   I. Title.
PZ8.3.B425Mad 1977   [E]   77-23792
ISBN 0-14-050261-0

Printed in the United States of America

Set in Bodoni

In an old house in Paris that was
 covered with vines
Lived twelve little girls in two
 straight lines.
In two straight lines they broke
 their bread
And brushed their teeth and went
 to bed.
They left the house at half-past
 nine—
The smallest one was Madeline.
In another old house that stood
 next door
Lived the son of the Spanish
 Ambassador.
He was all alone; his parents were
 away;
He had no one with whom to play.
He asked, "Please come, I invite
 you all,
To a wonderful Gypsy Carnival."
And so—
  Dear reader—

Here we go!

Up and down and down and up—
They hoped the wheel would never stop.
Round and round; the children cried,
"Dear Miss Clavel, just one more ride!"

A sudden gust of wind,
A bolt of lightning,

Even the Rooster found it frightening.

The big wheel stops; the passengers land.

How fortunate there is a taxi stand!

"Hurry, children, off with these things!
 You'll eat in bed."
 Mrs. Murphy brings
 The soup of the evening; it is half-past nine.

"Good heavens, where is MADELINE?"

Poor Miss Clavel, how would she feel
If she knew that on top of the Ferris wheel,
In weather that turned from bad to rotten,
Pepito and Madeline had been forgotten?

Pepito said, "Don't be afraid.
I will climb down and get some aid."
It was downpouring more and more
As he knocked on the Gypsies' caravan door.

The Gypsy Mama with her umbrella went
And got some help in the circus tent.
With the aid of the strong man and the clown,
Madeline was safely taken down.

The Gypsy Mama tucked them in
And gave them potent medicine.

The big wheel was folded, and the tent.
They packed their wagons and away they went.
For Gypsies do not like to stay—
They only come to go away.

A bright new day—the sky is blue;
The storm is gone; the world is new.

This is the Castle of Fountainblue—
"All this, dear children, belongs to you."

How wonderful to float in a pool,
Watch other children go to school,

Never to have to brush your teeth,

And never—never—

To go to sleep.

The Gypsies taught them grace

And speed,

And how to ride

The circus steed.

Then Madeline said, "It's about time
We sent dear Miss Clavel a line."

Poor Miss Clavel—a shadow of her former self
From worrying, because, instead of twelve,
There were only eleven little girls—
Stopped brushing their curls
     And suddenly revived
      When the postal card arrived.
"Thank heaven," she said, "the children are well!
But dear, oh dear, they've forgotten how to spell."
She studied the postmark, and then fast and faster

They rushed to the scene of the disaster.

The Gypsy Mama didn't like at all
What she saw in her magic crystal ball.

The Gypsy Mama said, "How would you like to try on
This lovely costume of a lion?"

With a curved needle and some string
She sewed both the children in,
And nobody knew what was inside
The tough old lion's leathery hide.

This was a fascinating game.
Compared to this, all else was tame.

A circus lion earns his bread
By scaring people half to death.

And after doing that, he's fed.

And after that, he's put to bed.

A lovely dawn and all was well;

The lion roamed through wood and dell.
He smelled sweet flowers; he came to a farm;

He frightened the barnyard—

Intending no harm.

They saw a man and said, "Please help
Us to get out of this old pelt."

The man was a hunter; he took his gun;
He got to his feet and started to run.

Said the lion, "We'd better go back, for if we're not
In a zoo or circus, we'll surely be shot."

They got to the tent
In time for the show.

"Look," said Madeline,
"There in the first row—"

"Oh yes," said Pepito,
"There are people we know!"

"Dear Miss Clavel! at last we found you!
Please let us put our arms around you."

The Gypsy Mama sobbed her grief
Into her only handkerchief.

The strong man suddenly felt weak,
And tears were running down his cheek.
Even the poor clown had to cry
As the time came to say good-by.

The best part of a voyage—by plane,
By ship,

Or train—

Is when the trip is over and you are

Home again.

Here is a freshly laundered shirty—
It's better to be clean than dirty.

In two straight lines
They broke their bread
And brushed their teeth
And went to bed.

"Good night, little girls, thank the Lord you are well!
And now PLEASE go to sleep," said Miss Clavel.
And she turned out the light and closed the door—

And then she came back, just to count them once more!

LE PONT

D'AVIGNON